Grandpa Jack

Scarlet

The Matey M'Lad

Collect all six exciting adventures:

Scarlet SILVER

The Matey M'Lad

Original concept by Sarah McConnell
Written by Lucy Courtenay
Illustrations by Sarah McConnell

Hodder
Children's
Books

A division of Hachette Children's Books

ISBN: 978 0 340 98914 2 (HB)
ISBN: 978 0 340 95969 5 (PB)
Printed in Great Britain by
Clays Ltd, St Ives plc

The paper used in this book by Hodder Children's Books
is a natural recyclable product made from wood grown in
sustainable forests. The manufacturing processes conform to the
environmental regulations of the country of origin.
The hard coverboard is recycled.

Hodder Children's Books
a division of Hachette Children's Books
338 Euston Road, London NW1 3BH
Hodder Children's Books Australia,
Level 17/207 Kent Street, Sydney, NSW 2000
An Hachette UK Company
www.hachette.co.uk

Contents

The Storm

Lightning split the air over the Seven Seas. The sky was black. The wind moaned, the rain fell and waves rose all around like unfriendly mountains.

In the middle of the storm, a strange-looking pirate ship called *55 Ocean Drive* was struggling to stay afloat. It looked like a house, but with masts and tightly furled sails. Several tiles had blown off its roof, and its window boxes were a sea of mud and wet geraniums.

A small blonde pirate in a waterproof plastic pirate hat was standing at the ship's wheel. Her beaded plaits hung down like soggy string. A square green pendant bounced on the front of her pink mackintosh. Her eyes were bright, and possibly the wettest budgie in the world was sitting on her shoulder.

"Not much longer!" Scarlet Silver shouted. She heaved the wheel to avoid a wave that looked like a cliff. "The storm will blow itself out soon. Hold on tight, Cedric!"

A very small pirate clinging to the mainmast flipped open the visor on the space helmet he was wearing. Rain spattered his glasses. "Don't worry, Scarlet," Cedric bellowed over the wind.

"I've tied myself to the yardarm. Watch!"

Cedric let go of the mast. The wind blew him off his feet, and he swung wildly past Scarlet. "Whee!" he shouted.

"Cedric!" Scarlet groaned, battling with the wheel as the rain got heavier. "Stop kidding around!"

"Pieces of eight," said the wettest budgie in the world, giving a tiny budgie sneeze.

"Go below if you want, Bluebeard,"
Scarlet said, reaching up to pet her
budgie. "Lipstick's down there, helping
Mum, Dad, Grandpa Jack and One-Eyed
Scott with dinner. Parrots know that
storms and feathers don't mix."

Bluebeard shuffled his feet and, if
possible, looked even wetter.

The wind screeched through *55 Ocean
Drive*'s masts.

"Whoo!" Cedric roared, hurtling past
Scarlet on his rope swing. He was now
upside down.

A red-haired lady in glasses and a
flowery rainhat stuck her head out of a
porthole. "Dinner!" Lila Silver shouted.

An old pirate in a black eye patch and
matching rainhat stumped out of the
cabin and took the wheel. "Go get yer

dinner, kids," he growled. "Leave some chips for me."

"Thanks, One-Eyed Scott," Scarlet said. Fighting the storm had made her hungry. Catching Cedric as he flew past for a second time, Scarlet pulled him down to the deck. They both dashed for the cabin steps.

The cabin was warm and smelt of fried fish. Three people, a red parrot and a ginger cat looked up from the tiny cabin table as Scarlet, Bluebeard and Cedric clattered inside.

Scarlet and Cedric's mum Lila was tipping out chips, with Lipstick the parrot on her shoulder. Scarlet and Cedric's dad Melvin was serving up the fish (keeping it well away from Ralph the cat). Grandpa Jack was trying to open a tricky

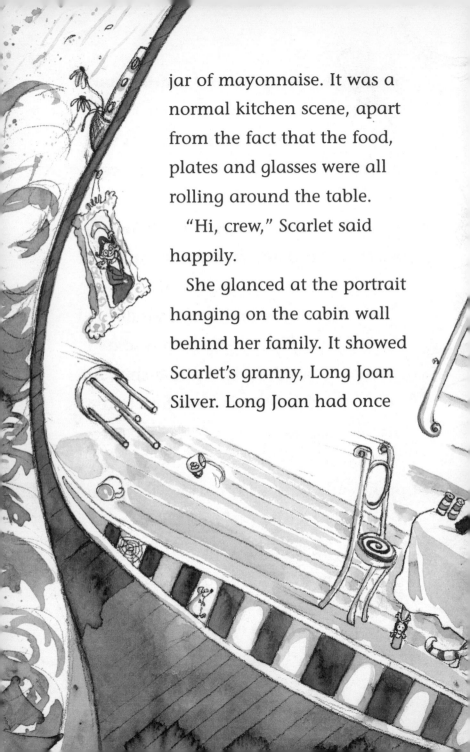

jar of mayonnaise. It was a normal kitchen scene, apart from the fact that the food, plates and glasses were all rolling around the table.

"Hi, crew," Scarlet said happily.

She glanced at the portrait hanging on the cabin wall behind her family. It showed Scarlet's granny, Long Joan Silver. Long Joan had once

been a famous pirate. Now
Scarlet was following in her
granny's footsteps.

Scarlet would never forget
the day that her family
realised they weren't just an
ordinary family but were, in
fact, real pirates. Since
Scarlet had been made
captain of the Silvers' old-
house-turned-pirate-ship, *55
Ocean Drive*, they had battled
the famous pirate Gilbert

Gauntlet twice, found Long Joan's old parrot Lipstick and heard his strange riddle about some tremendous treasure waiting to be found. Better still, they had worked out the first part of the riddle and found a puzzle piece, which would help lead them to it. Now they were just waiting for the storm to lift, before continuing on their treasure hunt.

"Sit down then," said Lila, waving a bottle of ketchup at Scarlet and Cedric. "Before your dinner goes cold."

Dinner was never very safe on board 55 Ocean Drive. With the storm, it was even worse. As Scarlet hung up her plastic pirate hat and mackintosh, the ship lurched sideways and a fork pronged into the floor. A knife clattered

to the ground and sliced an
escaping chip in half as the
ship lurched back again. One
of the cabin chairs tipped over

as a wave sloshed
across the deck overhead.
Ralph, who had been sitting
on the chair and trying to reach
the fish, fell off and slid under
the table.

Cedric was struggling to take off his space helmet. The heat in the cabin had fogged up his visor, and he kept banging into the furniture as he wrestled with the straps. He was crazy about space. Scarlet sometimes thought he would have preferred to be an astronaut, not a pirate at all.

"I'd like to drink a pirate toast to Granny," Scarlet said, seizing her glass of juice as it slid towards her and lifting it

up high. "May the giant shrimp who ate Long Joan Silver six years ago end up as someone else's dinner!"

"Ar!" cheered the crew.

"And may Granny's spirit watch over us on our tremendous treasure hunt!" Scarlet said, lifting her juice higher.

"Ar!" roared the crew again.

More chips rolled off everyone's plates. Ralph crept out from beneath the table and chased a few, thinking they were mice.

The storm was calmer by the time the Silvers had finished their dinner. Only one plate had been broken, which was a Silver record.

"Down to business," said Scarlet as Melvin put away the last of the drying-up. She took off her square green pendant and laid it on the table. Then she pulled out a piece of blue enamel with two straight edges and one wavy edge. She laid it on top of the pendant. It slid into one corner with a magnetic clunk.

"Underwater, overboard," Lipstick croaked at once. "Up on high and wave the sword. Solve the riddle at your leisure, come and find tremendous treasure."

"We have to find the next piece of this puzzle," Scarlet told her crew, "which means that we have to work out the second part of Lipstick's riddle: *overboard*."

"We solved the first part when we helped the Traffic Islanders escape from Gilbert Gauntlet through that underwater tunnel," Cedric said. "So I think we have to help someone who's fallen overboard this time."

"Plenty of people must have fallen overboard in the storm," Melvin said.

Everyone looked out of the portholes. The wind was still grumbling, but the waves were smaller and there was a peep of blue in the sky.

"Better hurry up and rescue 'em then," said One-Eyed Scott, who'd come inside and was now fiddling with the chicken bones tied in his scraggly black hair.

"Before a giant shrimp gets them too," said Grandpa Jack.

"There's no time to lose," Scarlet announced. "Let's set sail, crew! Look out for shipwrecks and people who've gone overboard. Our tremendous treasure is waiting!"

The Billboard

The sea was calm and the wind scudded *55 Ocean Drive* along. There was no sign of any shipwrecks, or people swimming around and needing to be rescued. There was hardly any sign that there'd been a storm at all. Scarlet sighed and adjusted the ship's wheel.

Perhaps the next part of the riddle won't be as easy as I'd hoped, she thought.

"Have you seen the colour of the water,

Scarlet?" asked Cedric, hanging over the edge of the ship. "It's fantastic!"

Scarlet glanced overboard. The water was the palest blue she had ever seen. She could see colourful fish darting underneath the ship, and sparkling sand lying in ridges on the seabed.

"Paradise," One-Eyed Scott sighed, holding his fishing rod with one hand and scratching his bottom with the other.

"Don't lean out so far, Cedric!" Lila called,

from where she was sitting tuning her accordion in the shade of the mainmast. "You might fall in."

"Maybe *I'm* the one who goes overboard," said Cedric cheerfully. He was now leaning so far over the ship's railings that his bottom was pointing up in the air. "Don't worry, Mum. I've fixed anchors to my leg splints."

He pulled himself back on-board and showed Lila his new gadgets. Both of the special splints he wore to help him walk had tiny steel anchors hanging down from them. The anchors were firmly wedged into the slots between the wooden planks on deck.

"Hmm," said Lila, doubtfully.

"Billboard ahoy!" shouted Melvin from up in the crow's nest.

"Bill who?" asked Grandpa Jack.

"Didn't we make 'im walk the plank once, Jack?" said One-Eyed Scott. "I 'ope he ain't back for revenge."

"Not Bill Board, you daft old dodgers,"
Melvin yelled. *"A billboard."*

The crew peered out to sea. Standing on
tall steel legs, an enormous billboard poked
out of the water. Plastered across it was a
bright purple and gold advertisement.

CALLING ALL OLD TIMERS!

Hanging up your cutlass, but still feeling sharp?
Bones a bit creaky, but still good for hornpipes till dawn?
Don't let the sun go down on you!
Spend your golden years aboard

THE MATEY M'LAD

Hot and cold running cabin boys in every room!
Resident pirate band, seafood chef and shipshape sunloungers!
Treasure hunts and pillaging expeditions ashore every weekend!

DON'T MISS THE BOAT!

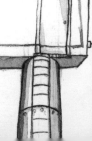

"Ooh," said Lila, laying aside her accordion in excitement. "I've heard of the *Matey M'Lad*. It's supposed to be the most glamorous pirate cruise ship on the Seven Seas. Strictly for old pirates, though. Like a retirement ship on water."

"I like the sound of the sunloungers," said Grandpa Jack.

"*Sunloungers*," One-Eyed Scott repeated, in a voice which made sunloungers sound like sewage. "You won't catch me on no sunlounger. I ain't never retiring, and that's that."

The legs of the billboard stood so high above the sea that *55 Ocean Drive* was able to sail right underneath it. It cast a long purple shadow across the pale blue water. Scarlet looked up at the bold purple and gold lettering and frowned.

Something about the advertisement
made her feel uneasy.

"I wonder if we'll see the *Matey M'Lad*
in these waters?" said Cedric sounding
excited. "I bet she's huge, with loads of
cannons and—"

Ralph shot out of the cabin, leaving a
trail of water behind him.

"Ralph, you're soaked!" Lila said, jumping to her feet.

"Bottoms!" Lipstick screeched as Ralph raced up the mast and showered the parrot with water.

Scarlet's heart flip-flopped. Wet cats on ships meant one thing.

A leak.

"Take the wheel, Mum!" she said, running for the cabin steps.

As soon as Scarlet set foot in the cabin, she felt water swirling around her ankles. She gasped. Water was leaking around the edges of *55 Ocean Drive*'s front door!

The trouble with having a pirate ship that had once been a house was the fact that it still had a front door. Half the door was below the water, and half the door was above. Of course, the Silvers had sealed it up as best they could. But the storm had battered the door so much that water was now seeping through Ralph's old cat flap.

"Head for the shore!" Scarlet shouted, tumbling out of the cabin. "We have to reach dry land before our front door breaks off its hinges and sends us all to the bottom of the sea!"

Silvertown

"Full speed ahead!" Scarlet shouted.

Lila, Melvin and Grandpa Jack passed buckets of water out of the soggy cabin to Cedric and One-Eyed Scott, who tipped them overboard. Lipstick and Bluebeard soared overhead and screeched encouragement.

"It's no good," Lila gasped, passing a bucket to Cedric. "It's coming in faster than we can bail it out!"

"Are we anywhere near land yet, Scarlet?" Melvin called.

Scarlet glanced at the chart beside the ship's wheel. "There's a string of islands called the Zimmers, just south-west of here," she said. "We'll be there in half an hour."

"Half an hour?" Grandpa Jack groaned, heaving another bucket of water up the cabin steps. "My back's killing me!"

"Best get into one of them *sunloungers* then," said One-Eyed Scott. "At least you'll be sitting quite comfortable when we sink."

Everyone kept bailing. Cedric found a length of hosepipe left over from the days when *55 Ocean Drive* had had a garden to water, which helped. Ralph sat up on the prow, and miaowed whenever he got splashed.

At last the Zimmers came into view: a row of islands like stepping stones set across the horizon. *55 Ocean Drive* was sitting so low in the water now that her hull was almost scraping the seabed. With the help of her crew, Scarlet lowered the ship's dinghy over the side. They tied *55 Ocean Drive* to the back of the dinghy,

seized the oars and towed it to the shore of the nearest island.

"We made it!" Scarlet panted as the dinghy bumped ashore just outside the island's harbour wall. *55 Ocean Drive* came to rest on the shallow seabed.

"Pieces of eight!" screeched Bluebeard from his usual position on Scarlet's hat.

A welcome sign in large-print letters stood on the harbour wall above them.

"Welcome to Silvertown, capital of the Zimmers," Scarlet read. *"The place to be when you've been everywhere else."*

The Silvers climbed up the harbour ladder and looked around.

Silvertown looked like an explosion in a florist's shop. Clashing floral curtains were draped in all the windows. Enormous beds of bright yellow and

orange flowers lined the quayside.
Hanging baskets of red and purple
flowers hung from the lamp-posts. The
benches around the harbour were
covered in squashy floral plastic and
looked like a row of waterproof sofas.

Sitting on the benches were rows and
rows of elderly pirates. Some of them
were asleep. Others were playing cards.
One of them was wearing an oxygen

mask attached to a tank beside him.
Most of them had ancient cats on their
laps or balding parrots on their
shoulders. Every now and then, they
would all look eagerly at the horizon.
Then their shoulders would slump and
they would go back to snoozing, or
tickling their pets.

"Hello?" said Scarlet.

A mutter went up along the benches.

"They've come! At last! Only two days
late ..."

Scarlet and her crew suddenly found
themselves surrounded. Ralph spat
fiercely at all the old cats from his
position on Melvin's head.

"Are you from the *Matey M'Lad*?" asked
a posh-sounding grey-haired pirate with
a shiny gold ring through his nose.

Scarlet shook her head. "Sorry," she said. "We've just come ashore to mend our front door."

A bone-thin old pirate whose orange hair was decorated with parrot feathers suddenly pushed out of the crowd.

"Chicken-Bones Scott!" she shouted. "It is, isn't it? I'd know that one eye anywhere!"

To Scarlet's amazement, One-Eyed Scott blushed. "Hello, Myrtle," he said.

"When did we last see each other?" Myrtle roared. "That time we stormed the old king's fort and stole all his gunpowder, wasn't it? Those were the days … And it can't be – Jumping Jack Silver?"

"Who is that, One-Eyed Scott?" Scarlet whispered as the orange-haired pirate kissed Grandpa Jack firmly on both cheeks, leaving two perfect pink lip-prints.

"Girl we used to know," One-Eyed Scott mumbled at the ground.

"Too bad about Joan," Myrtle was saying to Grandpa Jack. "Saw her just a little while back, it seems. Is this your family?"

Grandpa Jack introduced everyone. Myrtle tickled Cedric under the chin and swept Scarlet into a hug.

"You're the image of your granny," she said to Scarlet. "Captain, eh? Long Joan Silver is a tough act to follow."

"I know," said Scarlet. "I'm doing my best."

"That's the Silver spirit!" said Myrtle. She turned back to Grandpa Jack and One-Eyed Scott. "So," she said. "Come to sail away your twilight years on the *Matey M'Lad*, boys?"

"Is that why you're all here?" asked Melvin. "You're waiting for a trip on the *Matey M'Lad*?"

"Of course!" said Myrtle. "Saved up for years to buy myself a satin hammock aboard the pirate ship of my dreams. The ship was due here a couple of days ago. You didn't see it on your way, did you?"

The other old pirates looked hopefully

at Scarlet and her family.

There was a shout from the other side of the harbour.

"Something's coming!"

The pirates rushed away from Scarlet and her family, down to the water's edge. Several hats and a couple of walking sticks were thrown into the air. Suddenly,

everyone seemed to be waving tickets.

A shiny white speedboat with a golden hull zoomed into the harbour. Its engine roared as it came to a halt, sending up a plume of fizzing white water that drenched the floral benches.

"Ooooh!" shouted the excited pirates.

"That can't be the *Matey M'Lad*," said Lila, watching from a safe distance. "It's not big enough."

"Look what's written on the side!" Cedric said.

The Matey M'Lad Shuttle Service was painted in bright purple letters across the speedboat's golden hull.

"It's come to take the passengers to the ship," Melvin guessed.

"Flashy," One-Eyed Scott grunted.

Purple and gold, thought Scarlet. The colours had rung a bell when she had seen them out on the billboard. There was only one person on the Seven Seas who liked those colours and splashed them across everything he owned. But surely it couldn't be …

Scarlet shoved her family down behind
a floral bench as a familiar figure
bounded out of the speedboat's cabin.
The freshly pressed coat tails of his

pinstriped frock coat flew out as he
landed on the quay with his arms spread
out wide.

"My dear senior swashbucklers,"
Gilbert Gauntlet said, smiling his widest,
whitest smile. "How can I apologise
enough for my delay? Time simply flies
when one is polishing the twenty-four-
carat gold doorknobs that adorn that
Queen of the Seas, the *Matey M'Lad* ..."

Several pirates cheered.

"... shining up the solid oak decks ..."
More cheering followed this.

"... and retiling the fresh-water
swimming pool in precious gems!"
finished Gilbert Gauntlet.

This was followed by the loudest cheer
of all. Several pirates were beginning to
push each other out of the way in their

eagerness to board the speedboat.

"No need to push," Gilbert Gauntlet purred. "Plenty of room for all. Tickets if you please ... Now, step on board, and let me take you to Paradise!"

Shipwreck

"Gilbert Gauntlet!" Lila gasped in horror.

"He owns the *Matey M'Lad*?" Grandpa Jack said.

"That can't be good," said Cedric, shaking his head.

"Let me at 'im," One-Eyed Scott growled. "I'll tie his windpipe in a bow."

"No," Scarlet said, holding on to One-Eyed Scott's sleeve. "We've beaten him twice now, spoiling his sneaky scams. He won't be pleased to see us. We need to stay out of sight. If we want to find out what's going on with the *Matey M'Lad*, we have to follow that speedboat in secret!"

"But we've still got to fix the front door!" Melvin said.

"We've got everything we need on board," said Scarlet. She backed out from behind the bench. "Everyone, sneak back to the ship. It's low tide. *55 Ocean Drive* will be up on the dry sand now. If we're quick, we'll get it all fixed by the time that lot has boarded."

The speedboat was already filling up as the passengers moved down its golden gangplank. The Silvers and One-Eyed Scott shuffled backwards until they reached the edge of the harbour wall. Scarlet felt over the edge with the tips of her pointy green pirate boots with peacock tails embroidered down the sides. She found the harbour ladder and shinned down to where *55 Ocean Drive* lay peacefully on the sand. The others followed, with Lipstick and Bluebeard zooming silently overhead.

Cedric was the last to climb down the ladder.

"The speedboat's full already, and there's still loads of old pirates on the quay," he said, pulling the front door shut as he joined the others inside *55 Ocean Drive*. "How's Gilbert Gauntlet going to fit them all on-board?"

"Like sardines, I bet," said Scarlet.

Ralph miaowed at the mention of fish.

"Here's a hammer, Grandpa Jack," said Scarlet, handing out tools. "Dad? Nails.

Mum? You'll need to paint the joins of the door with tar when Dad and Grandpa Jack have finished mending the cat flap. One-Eyed Scott – there's still loads of water we have to bail out. And Cedric? Is there anything you can do to make *55 Ocean Drive* sail faster? We're going to need lots of whizz to keep up with that speedboat."

"By the time I've finished, *55 Ocean Drive* will be fast enough to zoom to the moon!" Cedric said enthusiastically. "I've invented a new hyperspeed sail and engine I've been dying to try out."

As Scarlet ran back and forth with tools for her crew, she couldn't help thinking about all the sneaky things Gilbert Gauntlet had done in the past. Back in his days as a builder, building a marina which had fallen into the sea. Running a pirate school that was nothing more than a factory of pirate slaves. Charging innocent islanders a heavy fee to leave their traffic-choked island. Scarlet and her crew had stopped him before. But could they do the same with the *Matey M'Lad*? They didn't even know what the problem was. Still, Scarlet felt sure there *was* a problem – somewhere.

At last, *55 Ocean Drive* was watertight again. Scarlet and her crew ran for the dinghy and towed their pirate ship into deeper water, keeping in the shadow of the harbour wall. Scarlet glanced back over her shoulder and gasped.

The speedboat was almost sinking under the weight of its passengers. Old pirates hung off the ropes around the deck. The pirate with the oxygen tank had been strapped to the cabin roof.

The speedboat's engine roared as it began to move.

"Wow!" Melvin gasped as the Silvers and One-Eyed Scott climbed back on board *55 Ocean Drive* and pulled up the dinghy. "That's fast!"

Despite its heavy load, the speedboat was almost out of sight already.

"Cedric!" Scarlet called. "Switch to full speed!"

Cedric flipped open a hatch on the deck and twiddled a couple of knobs. Streamlined sails fell down from the yardarm. He pressed a button. Somewhere down under the water, there was a roaring noise as *55 Ocean Drive's* new engine kicked into action.

"Wahoo!" called One-Eyed Scott, his chicken bones whipping around his head as *55 Ocean Drive* tore out into the open sea. "That's what I call sailing! Ouch," he added as one of his chicken bones whacked him in the eye.

The speedboat was still in sight, but only just.

"Has anyone fallen overboard yet, Dad?" Scarlet shouted up to the crow's nest, shading her eyes against the sun.

"No!" Melvin shouted back down. "The pirate on the cabin roof's lost his oxygen tank, though!"

55 Ocean Drive's engine choked and spluttered. The ship began to slow down.

"We're going to lose them!" Scarlet said. "What's happened, Cedric?"

"I'll take a look," Cedric replied, grabbing his tools. Attaching the little anchors on his splints to the railings, he lowered himself off the stern of the ship.

"The speedboat's nearly out of sight!" Melvin yelled from the crow's nest.

The sound of hammering drifted up

from the back of the ship. "I'm working
as fast as I can!" came Cedric's voice.
"It's a bit tricky when you're hanging
upside down ... Whoops, nearly lost my
glasses ... There!"

The engine spluttered back into life. One-Eyed Scott and Grandpa Jack hauled Cedric back on board as *55 Ocean Drive* leaped ahead again. But it was too late. The speedboat had vanished.

"We'll never catch him now," Cedric said, shaking his head.

"Bottoms," said Lipstick from his perch on the yardarm.

"Toasted toe-cheese," One-Eyed Scott grumbled.

"With mangy mustard," Melvin added.

The crew stared at the empty horizon. Everyone sighed.

"That gives me an idea for a song," said Lila suddenly, scrabbling around for her accordion.

Scarlet's crew sat down sadly on the deck and started humming the tune that

Lila was now playing on her accordion.

"This is no time for writing songs, Mum!" Scarlet shouted. Bluebeard flapped his wings hard on her hat. "Those old pirates need us! What if one of them falls overboard?"

"You saw how fast that speedboat was going, Scarlet," said Melvin. "The Seven Seas is a big place. We have no way of finding them."

"Tooo-asted toe-cheese," Lila crooned. "With maaangy muuustard …"

Scarlet stamped her foot. "Is this the family of Long Joan Silver or not?" she demanded. "Think of that poor old pirate who's lost his oxygen tank! And what about your so-called good friend Myrtle, One-Eyed Scott?"

Scarlet said *good friend* in a meaningful

voice. She had a feeling that Myrtle had once been someone special for the crotchety old pirate.

One-Eyed Scott blushed. He threw down his tambourine and got to his feet.

"Scarlet's right," he said. "We've got to keep trying."

"Look," said Lila, peering over the side of the ship. "The oxygen tank."

Grandpa Jack reeled the tank on-board with his fishing rod. Cedric pressed the engine booster button. *55 Ocean Drive* sprang forward like a speeding swordfish and raced onwards.

They were sailing among glittering silver sandbanks and tropical-looking islands now. There was no one around. The water shimmered, and the fish seemed to glow more brightly than ever.

"This really is a beautiful place," Melvin said, resting his chin on the railings and watching the fish as *55 Ocean Drive* sped along. "Those pirate pensioners probably don't need rescuing after all."

"I wouldn't be so sure about that," said Scarlet in a dark voice.

They had rounded a silvery sandbank and were zooming through a deep blue lagoon. Lying in the middle of the lagoon was a pitiful old ship. Its masts were splintered. Its sails were patched, and looked like they hadn't been washed in years. The bowsprit, which jutted out from the front of the ship, had snapped

in half. The figurehead was peeling
badly. Old cannons poked their rusty
noses out of their gunports like tortoises
peeping from their shells, and holes
gaped in the ship's sides.

A terrible moaning filled the air.

"What's that noise?" gasped Lila.

"It's the old pirates," said Scarlet grimly.

She pointed at the name painted on
the prow of the broken-down ship.

The *Matey M'Lad.*

Scuppered

"That's the *Matey M'Lad*?" said Lila faintly. "But where are the gold doorknobs? The solid oak decks? The gem-lined swimming pool?"

The Silvers and One-Eyed Scott stared at the old ship in front of them. It was little more than a wreck.

"I don't think it's got doors, let alone doorknobs," said Scarlet.

"The decks look holier than One-Eyed

Scott's socks," said Grandpa Jack.

"And there's no swimming pool," said Melvin. "Unless you count that broken washtub I can see on the deck."

The sound of wailing old pirates was dreadful. Scarlet couldn't stand it. She glanced around for signs of Gilbert Gauntlet's speedboat. A rippling wake spread from the *Matey M'Lad* to the horizon in the far distance.

"Gilbert Gauntlet's long gone," she said, pointing at the wake.

One-Eyed Scott said something so rude that a nearby dolphin leaping out of the clear blue water did a bellyflop.

"He's back!" shouted an angry voice from on board the *Matey M'Lad*. "That double-crossing dog-poo! Wait till I get my hands on you, Gauntlet ..."

A group of old pirates rushed to the side of the *Matey M'Lad* and stared across at *55 Ocean Drive*. Myrtle pushed through to the front.

"Is that you, Chicken-Bones?" she said, shading her eyes. "Jumping Jack?"

"We're here, Myrtle," said One-Eyed Scott in a deep voice. "We've come to rescue you!"

There was a feeble cheer from the old pirates as Scarlet guided *55 Ocean Drive* alongside the *Matey M'Lad*.

"I can't believe I fell for that mincing mogglestrap and his pretty words," Myrtle said furiously as she helped Scarlet and her family over the railings and on to the deck of the *Matey M'Lad*. "A pirate like me, with all my double-crossing experience! He got us all on-board with tales of making the ship look bad on the outside so that pirates – pirates other than us, I mean – wouldn't rob us. Then he zoomed off before we figured out his game. When I think of it – mind that plank there, dear, it's riddled with woodworm – it makes me madder than a mosquito with the measles!"

Melvin passed the oxygen tank over. It was seized gratefully by the wheezing old pirate who had lost it. The rest of the *Matey*

M'Lad's passengers crowded around and clapped Scarlet and her family on the back. Lipstick and Bluebeard flew up to perch on the yardarm with the other birds. Ralph chased a stupid looking rat underneath the mainmast and growled at a black cat with one eye that was sitting on the ship's railings.

"Is there a crew on board?" asked Scarlet, looking around.

"Of course not," said Myrtle. "We have to do everything ourselves. The water's too shallow to sail this ship ashore, and there's no rowing boats. The only running water on-board comes through the hull. The only bit of entertainment is a box of old knitting needles and a stack of broken fishing rods. All my life's stealings I spent on this place. And look at it!"

"We'll take you back to Silvertown," Lila offered at once.

To Scarlet's surprise, the pirates started protesting.

"I can't go back. My grandkids saved up specially for this place!"

"My wife died years ago, there's nothing for me back there ..."

"I sold me ship and cutlass ..."

"I ain't got nothing else!"

"But you can't stay here!" Melvin said.

Myrtle put her hand on One-Eyed Scott's arm. "She just needs a bit of fixing up," she said. "She was probably a fine old ship in her day, just like you and me was fine old pirates, Chicken-Bones. You'll help us, won't you? I ain't as young as I used to be."

One-Eyed Scott swelled up a bit.

"Nothing here that a lick of paint and a couple of nails won't fix," he said.

"Are you all right, One-Eyed Scott?" Lila asked, frowning. "You sound like you're catching a cold."

"We've got tools," said Scarlet. "A bit of spare timber, paint and nails and tar. I'm sure we can make the *Matey M'Lad* more comfortable for you. But are you sure you want to stay?"

"I can't show my face back home," said Myrtle. She patted the bright feathers in her hair. "I pinched these parrot feathers out of my son-in-law's best hat. He won't be best pleased to see me back again."

"Once a pirate, always a pirate, eh Myrtle?" One-Eyed Scott grinned.

Scarlet and her family rolled up their sleeves and set to work.

There was plenty to do.

One-Eyed Scott and Myrtle disappeared below deck with a bucket of tar and some nails to fix holes.

Cedric used his little leg-anchors as grappling hooks, and flung them over the yardarm so that he could pull himself up to mend the sails.

Melvin fixed the bowsprit with the help of some of the more active pirate pensioners, and gave the broken figurehead a fresh coat of paint.

Grandpa Jack mended all the broken fishing rods and swapped fishing tactics with the posh gold-nose-ringed pirate.

The more elderly pirates sat around with battered old instruments, playing pirate classics such as *Peg that Ole Leg Down* to keep everyone's spirits up. As they played,

Scarlet tied polishing rags to everyone's feet and got them to dance until the old deck looked shiny as a penny.

Lila bustled around in the dingy kitchen, boiling up a saucepan to make hot cups of tea in between playing verses of *The Groovy Groat*.

Ralph and the other cats chased hundreds of rats around the ship. And Lipstick and Bluebeard exchanged insults with the other parrots on the yardarm.

As the sun began to sink, Scarlet looked around at the results of their hard work. The *Matey M'Lad* looked pretty good for a broken old boat.

"Not bad," said Scarlet, to the gentle background *plop* of another rat being chased off the deck by Ralph and his friends. But she couldn't help feeling that it wasn't the paradise the old pirates had been promised.

One-Eyed Scott and Myrtle appeared on the cabin steps. Myrtle was blushing and One-Eyed Scott had a pink lipstick mark on his cheek.

"Bit of water coming in down below," One-Eyed Scott said. "Think you'd better come and take a look, Scarlet."

Scarlet followed One-Eyed Scott and Myrtle down the cabin steps, then down

again until they reached the ship's hold.
Water was bubbling up through a
patched hole right in the middle of the
floor.

"That's not good," said Scarlet.

She crouched down to get a better look.
Then she gasped.

The hole had been patched with a
piece of blue enamel, straight-edged on
two sides and wavy-edged on one side. It
looked like it might just fit in one of the
corners of her green pendant.

"It's another puzzle piece!" Scarlet cried.

She reached for it eagerly. Then she
stopped. If she took it out of the hole, the
Matey M'Lad would sink. But if she left it
where it was, how would they ever solve
Lipstick's riddle about the tremendous
treasure?

Paradise

"I've gathered everyone here to talk about something important," Scarlet said, standing in front of all the old pirates.

"Speak up!" called a pirate at the back. "I've had seawater in me ears for more 'n forty years!"

"My family and I are on a mission," Scarlet shouted. "A mission to find something that my grandmother, Long Joan Silver, left to us."

"Long Joan!" murmured the pirates.
"She had eyelashes that put a tarantula
to shame ..."

"She was always one for missions ..."

Scarlet hesitated. She didn't want to say
too much about the tremendous treasure.
After all, she was talking to the oldest

pirates in the business. What if they wanted a bit of the treasure for themselves?

"To find what we're looking for," she said carefully, "we need to collect the pieces of a puzzle. And we've found one aboard the *Matey M'Lad*. We want to take it, but—"

"Take it!" the pirates cried at once. "What are you waiting for?"

"It ain't that simple, shipmates," One-Eyed Scott said, coming to stand next to Scarlet and twiddling his chicken bones. "It's plugging a hole in the bottom of this ship. If we takes it, there's a chance that the *Matey M'Lad*'s headed for Davy Jones' Locker."

"Don't be silly, One-Eyed Scott," Lila said. "This David Jones person could never fit a whole ship in his locker."

"Mum," Cedric groaned as the old pirates roared with laughter. "Davy Jones' Locker is what pirates call the bottom of the sea. You're *so* embarrassing sometimes."

"Ain't there nothing you can do to stop the ship from sinking?" wheezed out the old pirate with the oxygen tank.

"We don't know without trying," Scarlet

said. "We want to know what you think."

"I think you should do it," said Myrtle. "We'll all stand by with nails and corks and whatever we can find to plug the hole. Let's take a chance, in the name of Long Joan Silver!"

"Aye!" roared the old pirates.

"Give it a try!"

"We need a bit of excitement!"

"Right," said Scarlet. "Follow me, everyone. Down to the hold!"

The hold of the *Matey M'Lad* was damp and nasty. Even Scarlet and her crew's best efforts hadn't made much difference down here, where the wood smelt rotten and beetles scuttled about. Scarlet knelt down beside the piece of blue enamel.

"Ready?" she said.

"Go!" roared the pirates.

Pop.

Scarlet jumped back, clutching the
puzzle piece as the water shot up like
a fountain.

"Overboard!" said Lipstick.

"I think Lipstick's got the right idea,"
spluttered Melvin, waving a plank

and nails in the air as the water poured through the hole. "I can't get near it!"

The sea was already past Scarlet's knees. The peacocks on her green pirate boots peered up at her through the rapidly rising water.

"Cork!" Scarlet shouted.

Lila tried to pass Scarlet a cork to plug the hole. But it bounced away on a wave of water.

"It's … coming in … too fast!" Scarlet gasped, washed back off her feet. "There's nothing … we can do!"

Lila grabbed Scarlet by the scruff of her pirate coat and dragged her up the ladder. Cedric had fixed two flipper gadgets to his leg splints, and was already swimming through the rising water like a seal. Melvin and Grandpa Jack and One-Eyed Scott tugged and heaved and pushed several large pirate bottoms up the hold's ladder to safety.

But already the water was rising through the next level of the *Matey M'Lad*. It roared through the holey old hammocks. It gushed out of the gunports. It drenched everything it touched. The *Matey M'Lad* was tilting – and sinking.

"Abandon ship!" Scarlet coughed, spitting out water. "Everyone overboard. Overboard! Swim for your lives!"

Plink! Plunk! Splat! Pirates, cats and parrots leaped overboard in a mass of billowing pirate coats, crutches and patched old bloomers. Some tried to use their bandanas as parachutes. The wheezy old pirate kicked his oxygen tank overboard and jumped on to it like a raft.

Behind the leaping pirates, the *Matey M'Lad* groaned and tilted further. With a whoosh, the whole ship broke in half and began to disappear under the sea.

"Get *off* my head, Ralph!" spluttered Melvin, striking out for the nearest sandbank.

Ralph ignored this. Instead he dug his

claws deeper into Melvin's hair and lifted his tail out of the water as Melvin struck out for land.

Cedric was zooming among the flailing pirates, pulling on their coat tails and kicking out with his super-speedy flippers, dragging them to safety one by one. Lila and Grandpa Jack had found the *Matey M'Lad*'s mast floating in the sea, and were coaxing old pirates to hold on while they towed it. One-Eyed Scott and Myrtle were clinging on to an old deckchair and kicking for all they were worth.

"I think that's everyone," Scarlet gasped at last, scanning the blue waters of the lagoon. "Mum?"

"All ashore," Lila coughed, treading water and trying to see through her sea-spattered glasses. "On that little island over there. Let's join them!"

The island was a pretty little place. Its waving green palm trees were heavy with coconuts. A stream sparkled in the sunlight, winding down through rocks to the lagoon.

Scarlet crawled out of the lagoon on to the pale pink sand of the island's curving beach. The *Matey M'Lad* was at the bottom of the sea. Now the old pirates had nowhere to go, and it was all her fault.

Grandpa Jack waded back out to sea, to gather all the fishing rods that were floating ashore. One-Eyed Scott had set up the deckchair, and he and Myrtle were sharing it. Melvin and Lila were helping pirates out of their wet clothes, and draping the clothes over the rocks to dry.

"I'm so sorry," Scarlet burst out, when

she had got her breath back. "I shouldn't have taken the puzzle piece out of the *Matey M'Lad*. Now you're all homeless!"

Myrtle squealed with laughter. Her

parrot feathers had already been laid out to dry on the pink sand beside her deckchair. "Best fun I've had since my old captain chased me up the mainmast!" she said. "Eh, Chicken-Bones?" And she slapped One-Eyed Scott on the leg.

"I feel ten years younger!" piped up the old pirate with the oxygen tank.

"There," said the posh gold-nose-ringed pirate, staring at his newly built palm-branch shelter with satisfaction. "Haven't made one of those in years, but I haven't lost the old touch."

Pots, pans, knitting needles and bits of torn sailcloth washed ashore behind Scarlet. Laughing and chatting, the old pirates began to gather everything up.

"We'll take you straight back to the Zimmers," Scarlet promised.

Myrtle sat up. "You'll do no such thing," she said. "This is Paradise!"

There were laughing faces everywhere Scarlet looked. A group of old lady pirates were sitting in the shade of a palm tree, weaving flowers through each other's wispy white hair. A group stood at the shore, studying the old *Matey M'Lad* fishing rods and chatting about the best spot to catch fish with Grandpa Jack. The old musicians were blowing the seawater out of their instruments and tuning up. One or two were even discussing diving trips around the wreck of the *Matey M'Lad* at the weekend.

"A great success once again, Captain," said Melvin, laying his hand on Scarlet's shoulder. "Well done."

"*Overboard*," Cedric giggled. "Too right, Granny!"

Scarlet pulled the little piece of blue enamel from her pocket. She took the pendant from her neck and laid the blue enamel neatly into a second corner. The magnets clicked together. Two pieces down. Two to go.

The merry crackling of a cooking fire filled the air. Scarlet could smell roasting fish and toasting coconuts. She gazed out at the rocking shape of *55 Ocean Drive* anchored peacefully in the lagoon.

"Let's stay here for a while," Cedric begged, stroking Ralph.

"Can we, Scarlet?" said Lila.

"The fishing's first rate," said Grandpa Jack happily.

"Sunloungers ain't so bad after all,"

said One-Eyed Scott, lying back in his deckchair with Myrtle on his knee.

Bluebeard gently nipped Scarlet's ear.

"I don't see why not," Scarlet grinned.

The tremendous treasure could wait a while. Scarlet kicked off her wet pirate boots to feel the silky sand between her toes as her crew cheered in delight.

"*Oh peg, peg that ole leg down,*" sang the pirate musicians in the soft island air.

"*Don't let it dance all by itself,*
Oh peg, peg that ole leg down,
Before it jiggles off the shelf,
That wood ain't broke,
That wood ain't dead,
It wants to twirl and twist and tread,
Oh peg, peg that ole leg down
Before it whacks you round the head!"

HB 978 0 340 98912 8
PB 978 0 340 95967 1

HB 978 0 340 98913 5
PB 978 0 340 95968 8

HB 978 0 340 98915 9
PB 978 0 340 95970 1

HB 978 0 340 98916 6
PB 978 0 340 95971 8

HB 978 0 340 98917 3
PB 978 0 340 95972 5

Read more of Scarlet Silver's adventures on the High Seas

Mum and Dad

Cedric

One-Eyed Sc